PICTURE BOOK   WAREHOUSE POINT LIBRARY

W9-BDG-525

✗

JE   JRECATJl2
398.8   Koontz, Robin Micha
Koo   Pussycat ate the
        dumplings

PUSSYCAT ATE
THE DUMPLINGS

PUSSYCAT ATE THE DUMPLINGS

Cat Rhymes from Mother Goose

Compiled and illustrated by
ROBIN MICHAL KOONTZ

DODD, MEAD & COMPANY • New York

WAREHOUSE POINT LIBRARY

Grateful acknowledgment to my family and friends, with special thanks for J.A.D., Rosanne, the Eugene City Library, and to Underfoot for her feline inspiration.

ARTIST'S NOTE

Mother Goose is not one person, but a name that represents traditional rhymes, verses, and songs that date back for centuries, as mothers have soothed their young ones with the same nursery rhymes that they heard as children.

Copyright © 1987 by Robin Michal Koontz
All rights reserved
No part of this book may be reproduced in any form
without permission in writing from the publisher
Distributed in Canada by
McClelland and Stewart Limited, Toronto
Printed in Hong Kong by South China Printing Company

1 2 3 4 5 6 7 8 9 10

Designed by Charlotte Staub

Library of Congress Cataloging-in-Publication Data

Pussycat ate the dumplings.

Summary: A collection of Mother Goose rhymes
involving cats.
1. Nursery rhymes. 2. Cats—Juvenile poetry.
3. Children's poetry. (1. Nursery rhymes. 2. Cats—
Poetry) I. Koontz, Robin Michal, ill.
PZ8.3.P9796 1987   398'.8   86-11671
ISBN 0-396-08899-6

Dedicated with love
to Virginia Koontz, my mom

I love little pussy,
  Her coat is so warm,
And if I don't hurt her,
  She'll do me no harm.
So I'll not pull her tail,
  Nor drive her away,
But pussy and I
  Very gently will play.
She shall sit by my side,
  And I'll give her some food;
And pussy will love me
  Because I am good.

Diddledy, diddledy, dumpty;
The cat ran up the plum tree.
    Half a crown
    To fetch her down;
Diddledy, diddledy, dumpty.

8

9

Two little kittens one stormy night,
Began to quarrel and then to fight;
One had a mouse, and the other had none,
And that's the way the quarrel begun.
    "I'll have that mouse," said the biggest cat.
    "You'll have that mouse? We'll see about that!"
    "I will have that mouse," said the eldest son.
    "You shan't have the mouse," said the little one.
I told you before 'twas a stormy night
When these two little kittens began to fight;
The old woman seized her sweeping broom,
And swept the two kittens right out of the room.
    The ground was covered with frost and snow,
    And the two little kittens had nowhere to go;
    So they laid them down on the mat at the door,
    While the old woman finished sweeping the floor.
Then they crept in, as quiet as mice,
All wet with the snow, and cold as ice,
For they found it was better, that stormy night,
To lie down and sleep than to quarrel and fight.

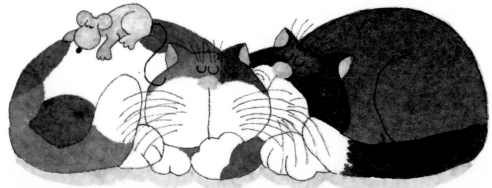

11

Ride away, ride away,
Johnny shall ride,
He shall have a pussycat
Tied to one side;

He shall have a little dog
Tied to the other,
And Johnny shall ride
To see his grandmother.

14

My pussycat
Has got the gout,
And the rats and mice
Can play about.

Pussycat ate the dumplings, the
 dumplings,
Pussycat ate the dumplings.
Mamma stood by, and cried,
 "Oh, fie!
Why did you eat the dumplings?"

17

Six little mice sat down to spin;
Pussy passed by and she peeped in.
What are you doing, my little men?
Weaving coats for gentlemen.
Shall I come in and cut off your
    threads?
No, no, Mistress Pussy, you'd bite
    off our heads.
Oh, no, I'll not; I'll help you to spin.
That may be so, but you can't come in.
Says Puss: You look so wondrous wise,
I like your whiskers and bright black
    eyes;
Your house is the nicest house I see,
I think there is room for you and for me.
The mice were so pleased that they
    opened the door,
and Pussy soon had them all dead
    on the floor.

Kitten, kitten, in my lap,
Now be good, and eat your pap.
We'll have a nightcap for your head,
And put you in the trundle bed.

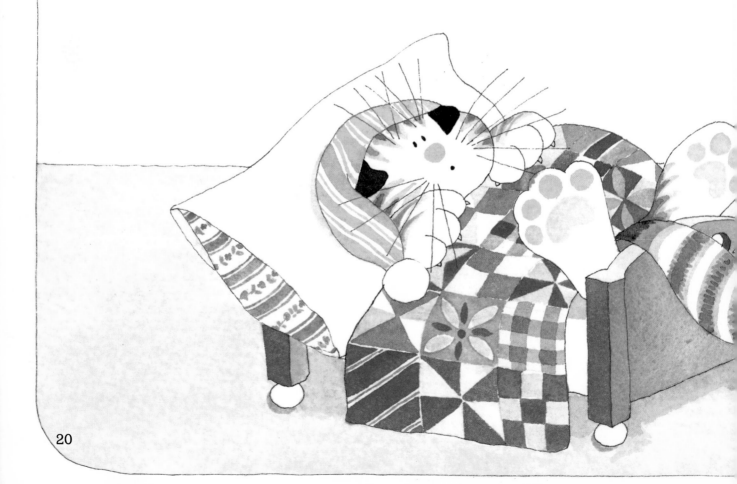

A cat came fiddling out of a barn,
With a pair of bagpipes under her arm;
She could sing nothing but fiddle-de-dee,
The mouse has married the bumblebee;
Pipe, cat—dance, mouse—
We'll have a wedding at our good house.

22

23

There once were two cats of Kilkenny,
Each thought there was one cat too many,

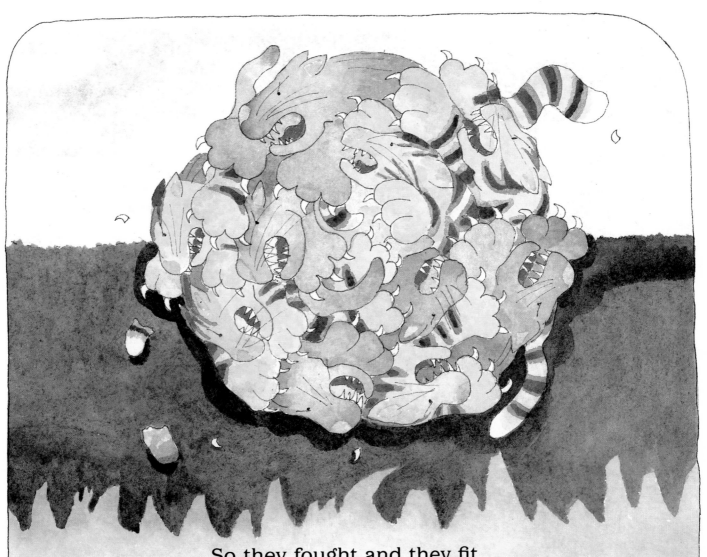

So they fought and they fit,
And they scratched and they bit,
Till, excepting their nails
And the tips of their tails,
Instead of two cats, there weren't any.

As I was going to St. Ives,
I met a man with seven wives,
Every wife had seven sacks,
Every sack had seven cats,
Every cat had seven kits:
Kits, cats, sacks, and wives
How many were there going to
St. Ives?

Answer: One.

26

There was an old woman
who lived in a hat,
Her only companion was
Grom-skin the cat:

And where she got victuals
and where she got drink,
Has puzzled the neighbors
to say or to think.

"Pussycat, pussycat,
Where have you been?"

"I've been to London
To look at the Queen."

"Pussycat, pussycat,
What did you there?"

"I frightened a little mouse
Under the chair."

A black-nosed kitten
will slumber all day,
A white-nosed kitten
is ever glad to play,

A yellow-nosed kitten
   will answer to your call,
And a gray-nosed kitten
   I wouldn't have at all.

Little Robin Redbreast sat
    upon a rail;
Niddle-naddle went his head,
    wiggle-waggle went his tail.
Little Robin Redbreast sat
    upon a tree,

Up went pussycat, and down
    went he;
Down came pussycat, and
    away Robin ran;
Says Little Robin Redbreast,
    "Catch me if you can."

Little Robin Redbreast jumped
    upon a wall;
Pussycat jumped after him,
    and almost got a fall.

Little Robin chirped and sang,
    and what did Pussy say?
Pussycat said, "Mew," and
    Robin jumped away.

35

Ding, dong, bell,
Pussy's in the well.
Who put her in?
Little Tommy Green.
Who pulled her out?
Little Tommy Stout.
What a naughty boy was that
To try and drown poor pussycat,
Who never did him any harm,
But killed the mice in father's barn.

Jack Sprat
Had a cat,
It had but one ear;
It went to buy butter
When butter was dear.

Dame Trot and her cat
Led a peaceable life,
When they were not troubled
With other folks' strife.
When Dame had her dinner
Near, pussy would wait.
And was sure to receive
A nice piece from her plate.

The cats went out to serenade,
And on a banjo sweetly played;
And summer nights they climbed a tree,
And sang, "My love, oh, come to me!"

43

Who's that ringing at my door bell?
A little pussycat that isn't very well.

Rub its nose with a little mutton fat,
That's the best cure for a little pussycat.

There was an old woman who rode on a broom,
With a high gee ho, gee humble;
And she took her old cat behind for a groom,
With a bimble, bamble, bumble—
They traveled along till they came to the sky,
With a high gee ho, gee humble;
But the journey so long made them very hungry,
With a bimble, bamble, bumble—
Says her cat, "I can't find something here to eat,
With a high gee ho, gee humble;

So let's go back again, I entreat,
With a bimble, bamble, bumble—"
The old woman would not go back so soon,
With a high gee ho, gee humble;
For she wanted to visit the Man in the Moon,
With a bimble, bamble, bumble—
Says the cat, "I'll go back myself to our house,
With a high gee ho, gee humble;
For there I can catch a good rat or a mouse,
With a bimble, bamble, bumble."

the end.